Oh, the things my mom will do...

because she loves me
through and through!

Marianne Richmond

sourcebooks
jabberwocky

Copyright © 2013 by Marianne Richmond
Cover and internal design © 2013 by Sourcebooks, Inc.
Cover and internal illustrations by Marianne Richmond
Cover design by Krista Joy Johnson/Sourcebooks, Inc.

Sourcebooks and the colophon are registered trademarks of Sourcebooks, Inc.

Published by Sourcebooks Jabberwocky, an imprint of Sourcebooks, Inc.
P.O. Box 4410, Naperville, Illinois 60567-4410
(630) 961-3900
Fax: (630) 961-2168
www.sourcebooks.com

Library of Congress Cataloging-in-Publication data is on file with the publisher.
Source of Production: Leo Paper, Heshan City, China
Date of Production: January 2013
Run Number: 19211

Printed and bound in China.
LEO 10 9 8 7 6 5 4 3 2 1

For CAJW, who can tell a few stories
about the things their mom will do...
all because I love them through and through!

Our family woke up late today.
The dog unplugged the clock.
The bus is honking up the street,
as I hurry down the block!

Honk!
Honk!

My mom is running after me

in her *pajamas* and *bare feet*.

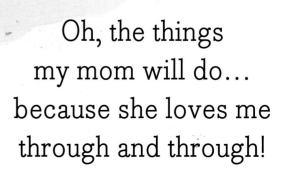

She hands my lunchbox to the driver as I fall into my seat!

Oh, the things
my mom will do…
because she loves me
through and through!

My head is feeling achy.
My tummy's icky sick.
I know what's gonna happen next.
"Mommm," I yell,
"come quick!"

She scoops me up inside the loop
between her arm and body,
then zooms me like a rocket
to land me at the potty.

Miss May picked me to be the frog
in our school's upcoming play.

Mom learns about my costume
with the show **one day away!**

She goes out shopping while I sleep,
then sews and glues with speed.
She's STILL sewing when I wake up
to finish what I need!

Oh, the things my mom will do...
because she loves me
through and through!

Welcome Moms

The Mother's Tea
is soon to start.
So far, MY mom's
not here.

She said her work
would end in time.
"I promise,"
she made clear.

I start to cry as lunch begins,
when—yippee—here she comes!
I don't see the speeding ticket
she's hiding as she runs.

Our pet hamster's cage is quiet.
I think he's feeling sick.
He's not making squeaky noises
or doing his best trick.

Mom makes her bed the pull-out couch
and wakes up 'round the clock

to feed him
orange juice
from a dropper
and rock him in
my sock!

VITA
C

The stormy thunder wakes me up
with a very loud
KA–BOOM!
It shakes the house and lights the night
and scares me in my room.

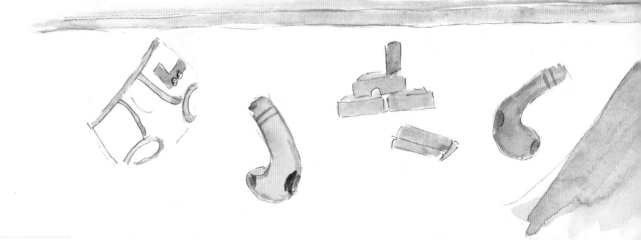

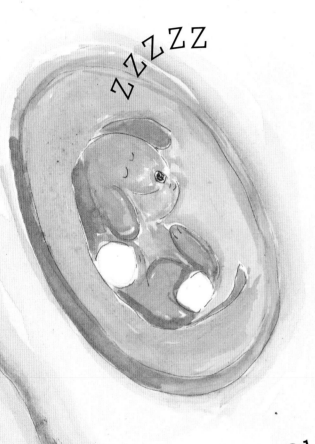

ZZZZZ

I wake up Mom and crawl in bed
and take the middle spot.
She hardly sleeps along her edge
'cause I kick and move A LOT!

Oh, the things my mom will do…
because she loves me
through and through!

Our family's busy every day.
Seems Mom is gone a lot.
She asks me please to understand.
I pretend,
but I do not.

CHORE CHART

Mom peeks her head into
my room and says,
"Let's go to Rocket Park!"

No cell phone or computer.

Just me and her 'til dark!

Me and Charlie go out back
to dig up worms and bugs.
We bring our new friends back inside
and spread them on Mom's rug!

She screams and drops
her laundry stack.
Her eyes grow big with fright.
Then she helps us build
a cardboard house
to keep them out of sight!

Oh, the things my mom will do...
because she loves me
through and through!

Me and Mom are
doing errands to
what seems like
everywhere,
when suddenly I
can't remember...

where I've left my Bear!

Mom forgets about our shopping and turns the car around.

We re-visit seven places until lost Bear is found!

The stars are twinkling in the sky
when Mom stops beside my bed

to pick up Bear from the floor
and put kisses on my head.

She sits down then in the stillness
and whispers in my ear.
I try real hard to act asleep,
and this is what I hear.

"I hope you know how much you're loved.
Yes, through and *through*
and THROUGH.
And, no matter what the days do bring,

I'll do anything for you!"

Also available from author & illustrator Marianne Richmond:

[9]